Common Core Lessons & Activities:
Heredity & Genetics

By Carole Marsh

Published by Gallopade International, Inc.

Printed in the U.S.A. (Peachtree City, Georgia)

TABLE OF CONTENTS

G: Includes Graphic Organizer

GO: Graphic Organizer is also available 8½" x
download at www.gallopade.com/client/g
(numbers above correspond to the graphic organi

What Is Heredity?

Read the text and answer the questions.

How would you describe yourself? For starters, you could describe yourself by what you look like. Are you tall, short, or medium height? Do you have blue, brown, green, or hazel eyes? Perhaps your eyes are a combination of colors! What color is your hair? Do you have short or long fingers? These noticeable features are called physical traits.

Have you ever wondered where these physical traits come from? The answer is you inherited traits from your parents. Heredity is the passing of traits from a parent to its offspring. Parents pass traits to their children through genes. Genes are the basic unit of heredity. Genes from your parents tell your body how it should grow, how it should function, and how it should look.

Heredity explains many natural patterns and why children often look like their parents. Heredity is why some people might say, "You have your mother's eyes" or "You smile just like your father." Heredity also explains why cats give birth to kittens and never to puppies. The traits of each living thing are passed through heredity.

1. A. Define physical traits as it is used in the text.
   B. Make inferences to list at least 5 ways to describe yourself.
2. A. Define heredity as it is used in the text.
   B. What is the relationship between genes and heredity?
3. What is the function of genes in your body?
4. Match each question to whether it is best answered by paragraph 1, 2, or 3 of the text.

   A) _____ What natural patterns does heredity explain?
   B) _____ How is heredity passed from parent to offspring?
   C) _____ How might I describe my physical traits?
5. With a partner, create a Venn diagram to compare and contrast your physical traits with your partner's. (Include traits like hair color, height, eye color, etc.)

Traits

Read the text and answer the questions.

A trait is a noticeable feature or characteristic in a living organism. Each living organism has a different combination of traits that makes it unique. That means that you look the way you look because you are a unique combination of traits. There are two main types of traits—physical traits and behavioral traits.

Physical traits are traits that determine your physical make-up. These traits include your height, hair color, eye shape, and many other physical qualities.

Behavioral traits are traits that determine the way a living organism acts, or behaves. For example, a mammal takes care of its young. This act of caring for its young is a behavioral trait.

Some traits are inherited, or passed from parent to offspring, and some traits are caused by an organism's environment. For example, you have inherited your hair color from your parents. But, because you stayed out in the sun too long, your hair might be lighter than normal. As another example, think about a pet animal. A cat might be naturally skinny (trait inherited), but if you feed it too much, it might become overweight (trait caused by environment).

1. Complete the table by summarizing details from each paragraph.

What are traits? Describe one of your own traits.	
What are the two kinds of traits? Give an example of each.	
What two things can determine traits? Give an example of each.	

2. Use the text to determine whether each trait is **physical** or **behavioral**.
   A. __________ An alligator does not take care of its young.
   B. __________ An alligator has cold blood.
   C. __________ An alligator has sharp teeth for hunting animals.
   D. __________ An alligator stays very still during the day
   E. __________ An alligator hunts for its food.

Passing It On

Read the text, look at the photographs, and answer the questions.

An animal's offspring typically resembles its parent. Through heredity, a parent gives its offspring many important physical characteristics such as fur color, tooth shape, body shape, and many other qualities.

Black Bear

Polar Bear

Fennec Fox

Red Fox

A

B

C

D

1. Match each parent to its offspring by identifying their similar traits.

Parent	Offspring	Similarities
Black Bear		
Polar Bear		
Fennec Fox		
Red Fox		

2. What physical characteristics separate polar bears from black bears?
3. What physical characteristics separate the fennec fox from the red fox?

Class Survey

Follow the instructions for parts A, B, and C.

PART A: As a class, take a survey on students' physical traits.

A. I am a	*male*	*female*
B. I can roll my tongue	*Yes*	*No*
C. I have attached earlobes	*Yes*	*No*
D. I have dimples	*Yes*	*No*
E. I have freckles	*Yes*	*No*
F. I have naturally straight hair	*Yes*	*No*

PART B: Complete the chart by collecting survey data from your class.

Physical Traits	Number of Students	% of Total Class
Males		
Females		
Can roll tongue		
Cannot roll tongue		
Attached earlobes		
Detached earlobes		
Dimples		
No dimples		
Freckles		
No freckles		
Straight hair		
Curly/Wavy hair		

PART C: Use the chart to answer the questions.

1. A. What is the purpose of a survey?
   B. Which trait was most common? Which trait was least common?
2. Use the data in the charts to make a bar graph of the traits. Label the x-axis "traits" and list the traits. Label y-axis "Number of people."
3. What is the benefit of viewing this information in a bar graph?
4. Determine whether each statement is **true** or **false**.
   A. _____ Your physical traits make you similar to other people.
   B. _____ Your physical traits make you different from other people.
   C. _____ Your physical traits make you unique.

Behaviors

Read the text and answer the questions.

Behaviors describe how an organism acts. Some behaviors are inherited and some are learned.

An inherited behavior is often called an "instinct," because it is natural and not learned. Think about types of dogs—a retriever is a type of dog that naturally has a desire to fetch. A shepherd is a type of dog that naturally has a desire to herd sheep. These natural desires, or "instincts," are not learned or taught. These are behavioral traits that animals inherit directly from their parents.

Some behaviors are learned. A dog does not naturally "play dead," but you can teach a dog to "play dead" on command. This is a learned behavior.

In your daily life, learned behaviors are often called "habits." Good habits often lead to positive benefits, and bad habits often lead to negative consequences. Eating healthy food every day is a habit that results in a good diet and good health. Eating junk food for lunch is habit which results in poor health. You might learn good habits in school, like studying to get good grades, or you might learn bad habits, like to misbehave.

1. A. Define behavior as it is used in the text.
   B. What is a synonym for inherited behaviors?
   C. What is a synonym for learned behaviors?

2. Use the text to determine whether each behavior is **inherited** or **learned**.
   A. __________ A bear is trained to perform in the circus.
   B. __________ Baby sea turtles instinctively go toward the sea.
   C. __________ A mouse naturally knows to avoid snakes.
   D. __________ A rat runs through a maze in 2 minutes. On its second time in the maze, it completes the maze in 1 minute.

3. A. Describe at least five bad habits you or your friends might have. Describe the consequences of each bad habit.
   B. Describe how you might change each bad habit to a good habit. What would be the result of changing your bad habit to a good habit?

Comparing Traits

Complete the graphic organizer by comparing physical traits and behavioral traits. Include examples and how each affects you.

Physical Traits **Behavioral Traits**

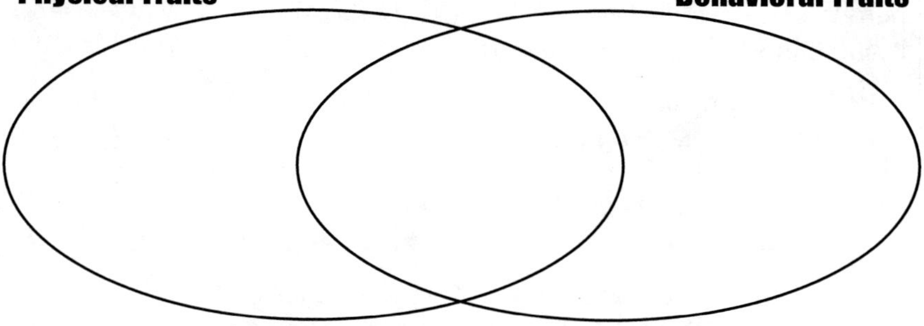

Identify each characteristic as either a physical or behavioral trait and as inherited or learned. Then explain how you reached your conclusions.

Trait	Behavioral or Physical	Inherited or Learned	Explanations
Liking the color red			
Wanting to eat vanilla ice cream			
Being tall			
Having green eyes			
Birds flying south in the fall			
Parents caring for their babies			
Having curly hair			
Watching television			

Mendel's Experiment

Read the text and answer the questions.

It is easy to see that children have many of the same traits as their parents. But, before the 1800s, no one understood *how* parents passed traits to their children. In the 1860s, an Austrian monk named Gregor Mendel made an important discovery.

While raising pea plants, Gregor Mendel observed that some pea plants were *tall*, and some were *short*. He saw that some pea plants produced *yellow* peas, while some produced *green* peas. And, some pea plants produced *smooth* peas while some produced *wrinkled* peas. Mendel wondered, "What causes these differences?"

To investigate the cause of these differences, Mendel planned an experiment. Mendel took a *tall* pea plant and cross-pollinated it with a *short* pea plant to see what kind of offspring they produced.

One *tall* parent and one *short* parent produced four *tall* offspring. "Strange," Mendel thought, "why did the trait for *tall* appear and the trait for *short* disappear?" He tried crossing a plant with *smooth* peas and a plant with *wrinkled* peas, which produced offspring with only smooth peas. When he crossed *green* pea plants with *yellow* pea plants, only *green* pea plants were produced.

Mendel concluded that each trait is controlled by two "invisible factors," called "alleles." An offspring gets one allele from each parent. Mendel also determined that one allele can mask, or cover up, the other. He called the allele that appeared "dominant" and the allele that disappeared "recessive."

1. A. What observations did Mendel make about pea plants?
   B. What question did Mendel ask based upon his observations?
   C. Describe Mendel's experiment with peas.
   D. What was the purpose of Mendel's experiment with peas?
   E. Describe the results of Mendel's experiments.
2. What conclusions did Mendel draw from his results?
3. A. What is the difference between "dominant" and "recessive"?
   B. In each experiment, which allele was dominant?
   Short or tall? Smooth or wrinkled? Yellow or green? Explain.

Punnett's Predictions

Read the texts, look at the diagrams, and answer the questions.

Genotype — the actual genetic make-up of an organism. In a Punnett's Square, genotype is described as a combination of two alleles – one allele from each parent. (Example: TT is a genotype that shows two Tall alleles)

Phenotype — an observable characteristic that results from the combination of two alleles in a genotype. (Example: being Tall or Short)

A Punnett's Square is used to predict the genotype of an offspring. It can also be used to predict the phenotype. It shows the probability of what alleles an offspring will get from its parents.

In the Punnett's Squares below, the shaded boxes represent the possible genotypes of the offspring.

Key: TT = dominant Tall (genotype Tall; phenotype Tall)
Tt = mixed (genotype Mixed; phenotype Tall)
tt = recessive Short (genotype Short; Phenotype Short)

Square 1		Alleles of Parent 2	
		t	t
Alleles of Parent 1	T	Tt	Tt
	T	Tt	Tt

Square 2		Alleles of Parent 2	
		T	t
Alleles of Parent 1	T	TT	Tt
	t	Tt	tt

1. A. What is the purpose of a Punnett's Square?
   B. What is the difference between a genotype and a phenotype?
   C. What is the relationship between genotype and phenotype?

Answer A-D for each of the two Punnett's Squares:
   A. List the possible genotypes of the offspring.
   B. How many offspring will have a short phenotype?
   C. How many offspring will have a tall phenotype?

3. Is it possible to carry an allele for "tallness" and be short? Explain.

4. **True** or **False**: In a mixed genotype, the dominant allele controls what phenotype appears. Explain, using evidence from above.

CAUSE & EFFECT

Genes

Read the text and answer the questions.

All living organisms are made of cells. The human body is made up of trillions of cells! Cells produce chemicals and proteins that organisms need to live. Cells also divide to create new cells.

How do cells know what to do? Genes! Genes tell a cell what proteins to make. Genes also control what type of cell is made when the cell divides. Most cells have a complete set of genes, but only some of the genes in a cell are "turned on." Genes are turned on and off at different times during development in order to make a bone cell look and act differently than a skin cell, for example. All cells—muscle cells, skin cells, brain cells, bone cells, and more—have specialized functions in the body.

Most organisms have two copies of every gene—one from the mother and one from the father. Specific combinations of genes determine hereditary traits, like height and eye color.

Genes store all the information a cell needs in their DNA. When a cell divides, it makes a copy of its DNA so the new cell has all the information it will need too!

1. Summarize the key information from the text to complete the graphic organizer.

What are Genes?		**Effects on**
	→	**Cells**
	→	**Heredity**
	→	**Cell Division**

2. Cells are called the "building blocks of life." Cite evidence from the text to explain and support this analogy.

PRIMARY SOURCE ANALYSIS

Nature? Nurture? Choice?

Read the quotations and summarize the point of view of each. Then answer the questions.

	Quotation:	Meaning:
1	"The precise form of an individual's activity is determined by the equipment with which he came into the world. In other words, it is determined by his heredity."	
2	"Our character is not so much the product of race and heredity as of those circumstances by which nature forms our habits, by which we are nurtured and live."	
3	"Life consists not simply in what heredity and environment do to us, but in what we make out of what they do to us."	

1. Indicate whether each statement below most supports the point of view expressed in Quotation 1, 2, or 3:
   A. _____ Parents should be held responsible for their child's actions.
   B. _____ A man with the best genes in the world will not do anything special if he wastes his talents.
   C. _____ Your genes are the single most important factor in determining who you are.
   D. _____ The environment you live in determines who you become.
   E. _____ Who you are is determined by the genes you inherit.
   F. _____ People can change.

2. Analyze the quote below. Describe the style and purpose of the quote. Determine which point of view it best matches, and explain your answer. *"We do not know, in most cases, how far social failure and success are due to heredity, and how far to environment. But environment is the easier of the two to improve." –J. B. S. Haldane*

3. Which quotation do you most agree with? Why? Use logical reasoning and personal experience to support your answer.

GRAPHIC ORGANIZER

Ideas about Genetics

Each table contains a list of common misconceptions about heredity and genetics. Use what you've learned to correct each misconception, and explain your reasoning.

Misconception	**Proper Conception**
Girls receive more hereditary information from their mothers, and boys receive more from their father.	
Personality is a trait that is passed from parent to child.	
Hereditary traits are passed through the blood. This is the meaning of "blood relative."	
Genes are the same thing as chromosomes.	
All physical traits are caused by genes.	
All mutations are harmful.	
Chromosomes are always present in a cell's nucleus.	
A genetic mutation can give you superhuman powers.	
All humans have the same genes.	

Explanation

DNA & RNA: The Keys to Life

Read the text look at the diagram, and answer the questions.

Cells contain two of the most important keys to life—DNA and RNA. **DNA** stands for **D**eoxyribo**n**ucleic **A**cid. DNA is the material that is responsible for copying and carrying genetic information. **RNA** stands for **R**ibo**n**ucleic **A**cid. RNA is the material that is responsible for carrying messages from DNA to the cell to make proteins.

DNA is a thin thread-like material that has two strands and looks like a twisted ladder. This twisted ladder shape is called a "double helix." The steps of this ladder are made up of four different chemicals called <u>nucleobases</u>—cytocine, guanine, adenine, and thymine. These four nucleobases bond together in pairs of two—adenine always bonds with thymine, and cytosine always bonds with guanine.

RNA is also thin and thread-like. However, RNA is single-stranded. Its shape is called a "helix." RNA looks like half of a ladder. RNA has three of the same nucleobases as DNA—cytosine, guanine, and adenine—and one that is different—uracil.

A cell contains a lot of DNA. A cell's DNA is tightly coiled into small units called chromosomes, located in a cell's nucleus. When two parents reproduce, each parent passes down exactly one-half of its chromosomes to the offspring. The two halves combine to give the offspring its complete DNA.

PART A: Use the text to answer the questions.

1. *An acronym is a word formed from the initial letters of other words.*
   A. <u>DNA</u> is an acronym for what genetic material?
   B <u>RNA</u> is an acronym for what genetic material?

2. Explain the functions of DNA and RNA.

Material	Function
DNA	
RNA	

3. Where does an offspring get its DNA?

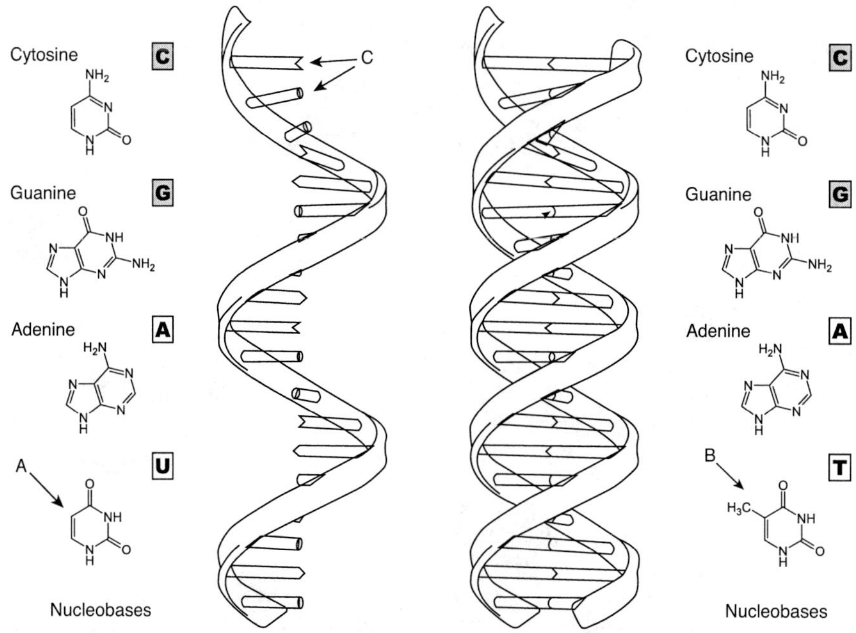

Diagram A **Diagram B**

PART B: Use the text and diagrams to answer the questions.

4. A. What is represented by Diagram A?
   B. What is the name of the shape of the item in Diagram A?
   C. What is represented by Diagram B?
   D. What is the name of the shape of the item in Diagram B?
5. A. What nucleobase does Arrow A point to?
   B. What nucleobase does Arrow B point to?
6. Use the Venn diagram to compare and contrast DNA and RNA.

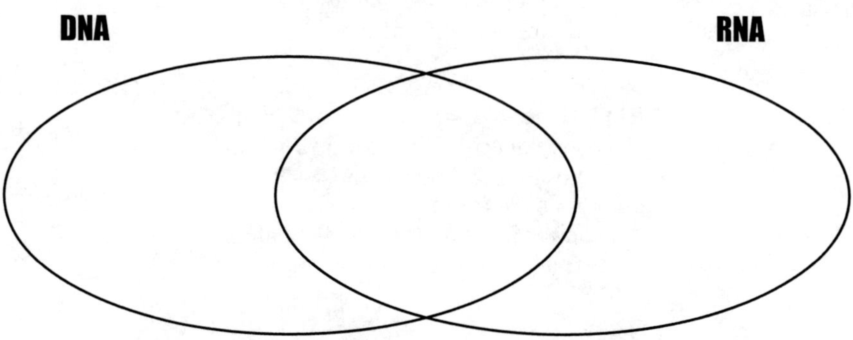

Mitosis

Read the observation and answer the questions.

Observation Report of Human Skin Cell Mitosis
Viewed under microscope magnification x300. July 3, 2013

12:02 A.M. The cell is in its normal resting state, called the interphase. There is no visible change in the cell. Inside, however, the nucleus is duplicating chromatin (DNA) and preparing for cell reproduction. This is also called mitosis.

5:31 A.M. Apparently, the nucleus envelope has dissolved and disappeared. The cell has entered the prophase of mitosis. The chromatin inside the nucleus begins clumping together into pairs of chromosomes. The chromosomes appear x-shaped. The cell's centrioles move to each end of the cell, and long, thin spider-like threads appear from the centrioles.

10:16 A.M. The spider-like threads, called spindles, have attached to the chromosomes and lined them up at the cell's center. The cells metaphase organizes the chromosomes for division. That way, each new cell gets exactly one copy of each chromosome.

2:41 P.M. The cell begins anaphase. The paired chromosomes separate in half. The spindle threads pull a copy of each chromosome to opposite ends of the cell.

7:56 P.M. The chromosomes at each end of the cell lose their shape and turn into chromatin. This must be the telophase. Two new nuclear envelopes form around the chromatin at each end of the cell. Two new nucleuses are being born! Spindle fibers slowly disappear.

11: 02 P.M. The cell forms a wall between the two nucleuses in cytokinesis. This wall slowly pinches the cell until it separates into two new cells. Each new "daughter " cell contains an exact copy of the DNA of the "parent" cell. Now each cell has all the genetic material necessary to reproduce again and again and again.

1. Use the text to define <u>mitosis</u>.
2. What is the purpose of mitosis?
3. What is the purpose of the text?
4. List 3-5 things you can you logically conclude about the person who wrote the text. Cite evidence from the text to support each response.
5. Why is a microscope required for observation of this process?
6. Use the text to number the sequence of events in the correct order.
   ______DNA is held in the nucleus as chromatin
   ______Two new nucleuses form, each with its own DNA copy
   ______Chromatin clumps into pairs of chromosomes
   ______The nucleus creates a copy of the DNA in chromatin
   ______Chromosome pairs divide into two identical sets
7. Use the text to identify each phase of mitosis. Then number the phases in the correct order in the boxes.

☐ ______________

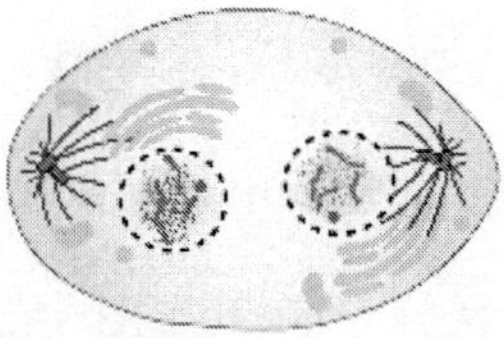

☐ ______________

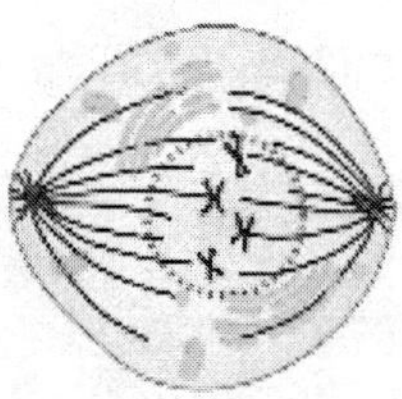

☐ ______________

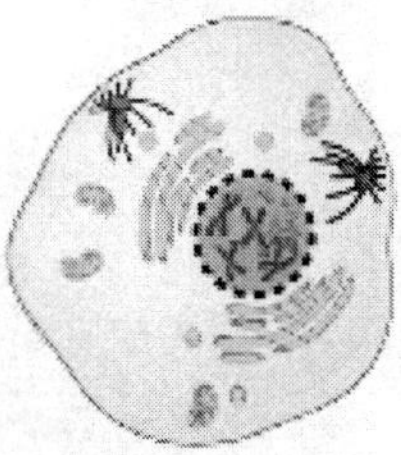

☐ ______________

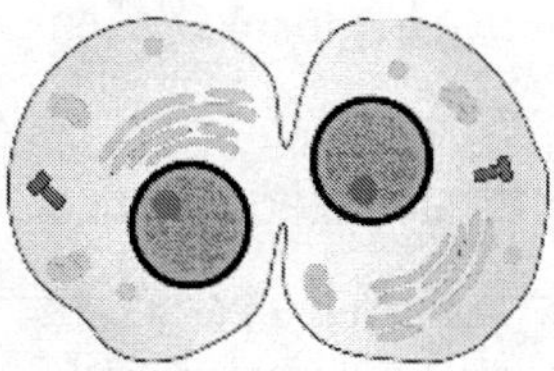

☐ ______________

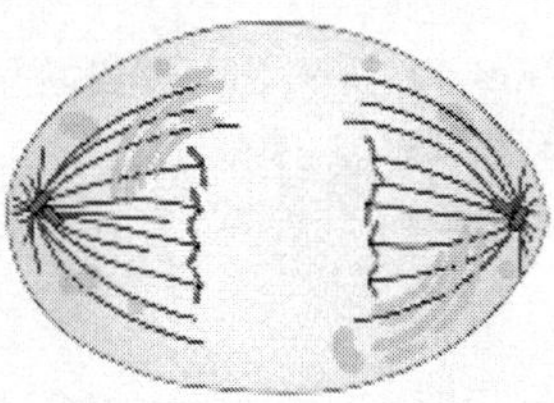

☐ ______________

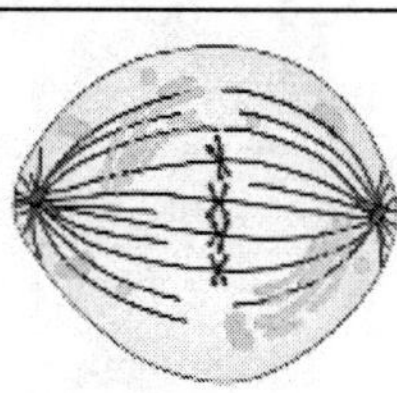

Genetic Disorders

PART A: Read the text and answer the questions.

A genetic disorder is a disease that is caused by a mistake in a person's DNA. During DNA replication, DNA can become changed or "mutated." A mutation occurs when the DNA does not make an exact copy of itself. A mutation can be as small as copying the wrong nucleobase or as large as completely missing a chromosome. Some genetic mutations are harmless, some are even beneficial, but some genetic mutations cause life-changing disorders.

Most genetic disorders are inherited. Remember, organisms have two alleles (genotype) for every trait (phenotype). They get one of each allele from each of their parents. If an organism inherits a mutated dominant allele, it can cause a genetic disorder. If two mutated recessive alleles are inherited, that can also cause a genetic disorder. There are other things, too, that cause genetic disorders, including exposure to certain chemicals, ultraviolet radiation from the sun, and other environmental factors.

Most people carry genetic mutations, but the mutation does not appear as a disorder. In many cases, an organism's cells will correct or fix a mutation. Also, if a mutation is found in a recessive allele, the disorder might not affect the person at all. However, a person who carries a genetic mutation, even if not affected, can pass the genetic disorder to his or her children.

1. A. Use the text to define genetic mutation.
2. A. What causes most genetic disorders?
   B. What are additional causes of genetic disorders?
3. Can you tell if a person has a genetic disorder just by looking at them? Explain why or why not.
4. For each question, indicate whether it is best answered by paragraph 1, 2, or 3. Then answer the questions.
   A. _____ What role does DNA play in producing genetic disorders?
   B. _____ Why can a genetic mutation be "invisible"?
   C. _____ Where do genetic disorders come from?

PART B: Read the text and answer the questions below.

1) **Abraham Lincoln**, the 16th president of the United States, was an extremely tall man for his time. He had a large jutting chin and drooping eyelids. President Lincoln also suffered from periods of deep depression. Lincoln's close friends and relatives worried about his mental health before and during his presidency.

2) **Alexei Nikolayevich** was the only son of Czar Nicholas II or Russia. Most children, if scraped or bruised, heal rather quickly. But, if Alexei fell and scraped his knee, his knee would bleed for days. A small bruise could swell and cover large parts of Alexei's body. Nicholas II was very careful to protect Alexei—the smallest injury could have meant death for the child.

3) **Albert Einstein** is one of the most brilliant scientists in history. However, many of Einstein's friends recall that he was often uncomfortable and awkward with people. He often isolated himself, working on his theories for very long periods of time.

4) **Frederic Chopin** was a 19th Century musical composer. He suffered from severe coughing most of his life. Many people thought that he had tuberculosis, a disease that attacks the lungs.

5. Identify which genetic disorder best describes the disorder of each historical figure in the text.
   A. _____ Asperger syndrome is characterized by difficulty with social interaction and nonverbal communication, as well as increased intelligence and an extreme interest and focus on one subject.
   B. _____ Hemophilia is characterized by a lack of platelets in the blood. Platelets are the part of the blood responsible for repairing torn skin and clotting wounds.
   C. _____ Marfan synodrome is a disease that affects tissue between muscles and bones. This disease causes unnatural growth and stretching of bones and muscles.
   D. _____ Cystic fibrosis is a disease that affects the liver, pancreas, and lungs. Cystic fibrosis most commonly leads to difficulty breathing and repeated infections in the respiratory system.

6. In your opinion, did any of these famous historic figures benefit from his genetic disorder? Write a short paragraph to support your opinion with evidence and with logical reasoning.

Blood Types

Look at the diagram and answer the questions.

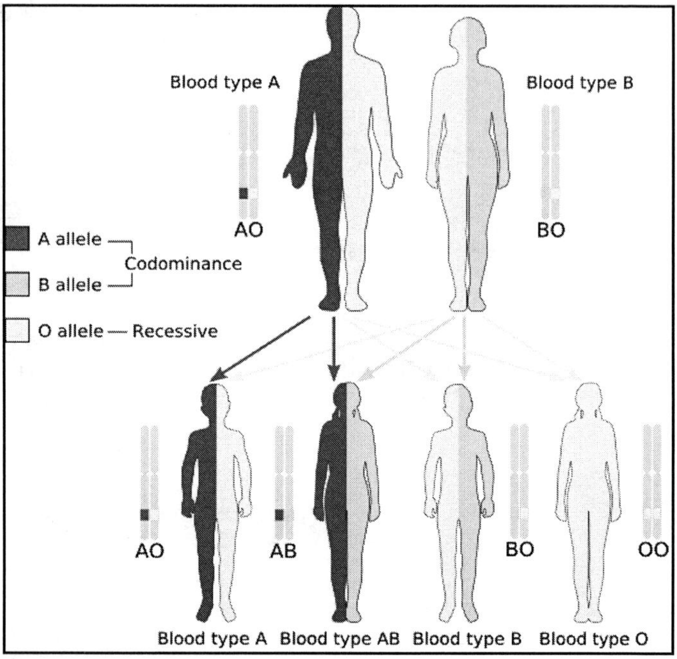

1. A. What is represented by the two large people at the top?
   B. What is represented by the four small people at the bottom?
   C. What is the purpose of the diagram?
2. A. How many different blood type alleles are shown in the diagram?
   B. How many blood type alleles does each offspring inherit?
3. A. What are the four genotypes shown in the diagram?
   B. What are the four phenotypes shown in the diagram?
4. "Codominance" occurs when a gene has more than one dominant allele. A person with two dominant alleles will express the phenotype of both. Which person or people in the diagram have codominance?

BONUS:

A. Are there more possible genotypes for blood type than the four shown in the diagram? Explain your response.
B. Are there more possible phenotypes for blood type than the four shown in the diagram? Explain your response.

Geneticists

Use online resources to complete the graphic organizer. Tell, "Who am I?" and "What did I do?"

People/ Organization	Who am I?	What did I do?
Gregor Mendel		
William Bateson		
Thomas Hunt Morgan		
James D. Watson and Francis Crick		
Frederick Sanger		
Human Genome Project		

Genetics in Use

Read the text and answer the questions.

Genetics is the branch of science that deals with heredity, particularly the transmission of genes and traits from parents to offspring. Genetics is extremely useful!

Genetics is used to improve the quality and quantity of our food supply. Plants geneticists may cross-breed plants to produce offspring that grow larger fruit, that are less susceptible to disease or drought, and that look or taste better. In animal science, geneticists help farmers choose the best cows, sheep, pigs, and chickens to breed in order to produce the best types of meat.

By researching and studying human genes, medical geneticists have been able to identify the alleles that cause many genetic disorders. Geneticists can test for many genetic disorders and predict the risk of two parents passing a genetic disorder to their children. Geneticists can also test for certain genes to find out if a person has a genetic order that increases their risk of developing a disease later in life. Geneticists can act as counselors, helping people make decisions about how to deal with genetic disorders.

Genetics is also useful in solving crimes. If a criminal leaves any small part of his or her hair, skin, blood, or other cells at the crime scene, a geneticist can test its genetic material to see if it matches the DNA of a suspect accused of committing the crime. This branch of science is called forensic science. Genetic evidence has been used in courts to help convict many criminals and to help many innocent people be found "not guilty."

1. A. What is the main idea of this text?
   B. Explain how each paragraph supports the main idea.

2. Explain the benefits of genetics in each branch of science.

Agriculture	Animal Science	Medicine	Forensics

Structures in Genetics

Use a dictionary or other resource to complete the table. Then use the information in the table to label the diagram.

Structure	Description	Function
cell		
chromosome		
DNA		
double helix		
nucleus		
nucleobases		

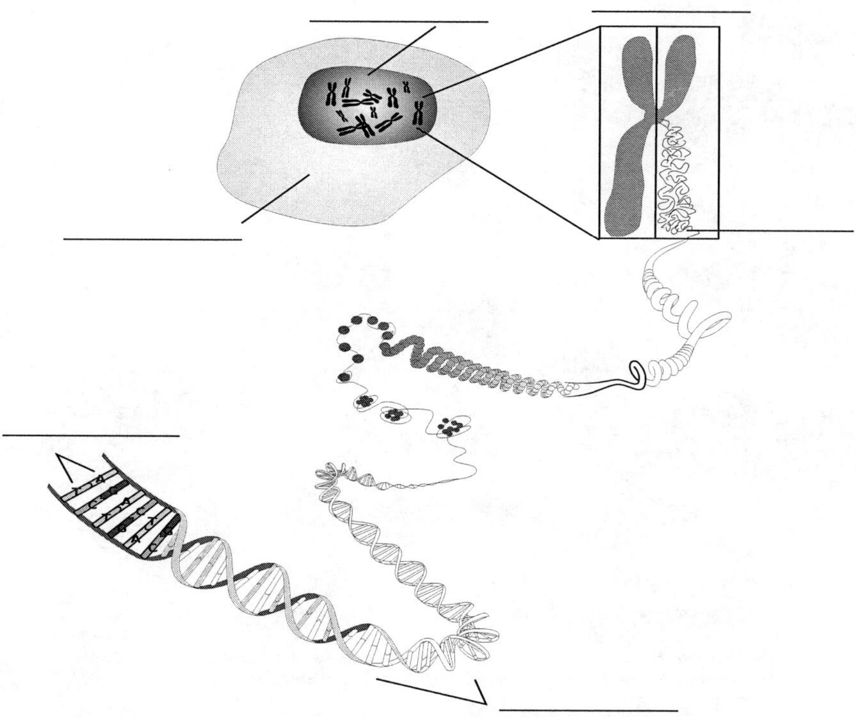

Correlations to Common Core State Standards

For your convenience, correlations are listed page-by-page, and for the entire book!

This book is correlated to the Common Core State Standards for English Language Arts grades 3-8, and to Common Core State Standards for Literacy in History, Science, & Technological Subjects grades 6-8.

Correlations are highlighted in gray.

	READING	WRITING	LANGUAGE	SPEAKING & LISTENING
	Includes: RI: Reading Informational Text RST: Reading Science & Technical Subjects	*Includes:* W: Writing WHST: Writing History/Social Studies, Science, & Technical Subjects	*Includes:* L: Language LF: Language Foundational Skills	*Includes:* SL: Speaking & Listening
PAGE #				
2	RI RST · **1 2 3 4 5** 6 7 **8** 9 **10**	W WHST · 1 **2** 3 **4 5** 6 7 **8 9 10**	L LF · 1 2 3 **4 5 6**	SL · **1** 2 3 4 5 6
3	RI RST · **1 2 3 4 5** 6 7 **8** 9 **10**	W WHST · 1 **2** 3 **4** 5 6 7 **8 9 10**	L LF · 1 2 3 **4** 5 **6**	SL · 1 2 3 4 5 6
4	RI RST · **1** 2 **3** 4 **5 6 7 8 9 10**	W WHST · 1 **2** 3 **4** 5 6 7 **8** 9 **10**	L LF · 1 2 3 4 5 6	SL · 1 2 3 4 5 6
5	RI RST · **1 2 3** 4 **5** 6 **7** 8 9 **10**	W WHST · 1 **2** 3 **4 5** 6 **7 8 9 10**	L LF · 1 2 3 4 5 6	SL · **1 2** 3 **4** 5 **6**
6	RI RST · **1 2 3 4 5** 6 7 **8** 9 **10**	W WHST · **1 2 3 4** 5 6 7 **8 9 10**	L LF · 1 2 3 **4 5 6**	SL · 1 2 3 4 5 6
7	RI RST · **1 2** 3 **4** 5 6 **7** 8 **9 10**	W WHST · 1 **2** 3 **4** 5 6 7 **8 9 10**	L LF · 1 2 3 **4** 5 **6**	SL · 1 2 3 4 5 6
8	RI RST · **1** 2 **3 4 5** 6 7 **8** 9 **10**	W WHST · 1 **2** 3 **4** 5 6 7 8 **9 10**	L LF · 1 2 3 **4** 5 **6**	SL · 1 2 3 4 5 6
9	RI RST · **1 2 3 4 5** 6 **7 8 9 10**	W WHST · 1 **2** 3 **4** 5 6 7 8 **9 10**	L LF · 1 2 3 **4** 5 **6**	SL · 1 2 3 4 5 6
10	RI RST · **1 2 3** 4 **5** 6 7 **8** 9 **10**	W WHST · 1 **2** 3 **4** 5 6 7 8 **9 10**	L LF · 1 2 3 **4 5 6**	SL · 1 2 3 4 5 6
11	RI RST · **1 2 3 4 5 6** 7 **8 9 10**	W WHST · **1 2** 3 **4 5** 6 7 **8 9 10**	L LF · 1 2 3 4 **5 6**	SL · 1 2 3 4 5 6
12-13	RI RST · **1** 2 **3** 4 5 **6** 7 **8 9 10**	W WHST · 1 **2** 3 **4** 5 6 7 **8 9 10**	L LF · 1 2 3 4 5 6	SL · 1 2 3 4 5 6
14-15	RI RST · **1 2 3 4 5 6 7 8 9 10**	W WHST · 1 **2** 3 **4** 5 6 7 **8 9 10**	L LF · 1 2 3 **4 5 6**	SL · 1 2 3 4 5 6
16-17	RI RST · **1 2 3 4 5 6 7 8** 9 **10**	W WHST · 1 **2** 3 4 5 6 7 **8 9 10**	L LF · 1 2 3 **4** 5 **6**	SL · 1 2 3 4 5 6
18-19	RI RST · **1** 2 **3 4 5** 6 7 **8 9 10**	W WHST · **1 2** 3 **4** 5 6 7 **8 9 10**	L LF · 1 2 3 **4** 5 **6**	SL · 1 2 3 4 5 6
20	RI RST · **1 2** 3 **4 5** 6 **7** 8 **9 10**	W WHST · 1 **2** 3 **4** 5 6 7 **8 9 10**	L LF · 1 2 3 **4** 5 **6**	SL · 1 2 3 4 5 6
21	RI RST · **1** 2 3 4 5 6 7 **8 9 10**	W WHST · 1 **2** 3 **4 5 6 7 8** 9 **10**	L LF · 1 2 3 4 5 6	SL · **1** 2 3 4 5 6
22	RI RST · **1 2 3** 4 **5** 6 7 **8** 9 **10**	W WHST · 1 **2** 3 **4** 5 6 7 8 **9 10**	L LF · 1 2 3 4 5 6	SL · 1 2 3 4 5 6
23	RI RST · 1 2 3 **4** 5 6 **7** 8 9 **10**	W WHST · 1 **2** 3 4 5 6 **7** 8 9 **10**	L LF · 1 2 3 **4 5 6**	SL · 1 2 3 4 5 6
COMPLETE BOOK	RI RST · **1 2 3 4 5 6 7 8 9 10**	W WHST · **1 2 3 4 5 6 7 8 9 10**	L LF · 1 2 3 **4 5 6**	SL · **1 2** 3 **4** 5 **6**

For the complete Common Core standard identifier, combine your grade + "." + letter code above + "." + number code above.

In addition to the correlations indicated here, the activities may be adapted or expanded to align to additional standards and to meet the diverse needs of your unique students!